Dragon Slayers' Academy ™ 2

REVENGE OF
THE DRAGON LADY

By Kate McMullan

Illustrated by Bill Basso

D0954175

GROSSET & DUNLAP • NEW YORK

For Jim, my darling boy

—K. McM.

Library of Congress Cataloging-in-Publication Data

McMullan, K.H.
    Revenge of the dragon lady / by K.H. McMullan ; illustrated by Bill Basso.
        p. cm. — (Dragon Slayers' Academy ; 2)
    Summary: After accidentally killing a dragon, Wiglaf hopes his friends at Dragon Slayers' Academy will be able to help him prove himself a hero when he faces that dragon's mother, Seetha, the Beast from the East.
        [1. Dragons—Fiction. 2. Schools—Fiction. 3. Courage—Fiction.]
    I. Basso, Bill, ill. II. Title. III. Series: McMullan, K.H.
    Dragon Slayers' Academy ; 2.
    PZ7.M47879Re 1997   97-31171
    [Fic]—dc21   CIP
                                                                                        AC

ISBN 0-448-43109-2   I J

Chapter I

Wiglaf sat in the cold dining hall of Dragon Slayers' Academy. He stared at the slimy jellied eels on his plate.

"Yuck!" he said to his friend Erica. "I'm sick of having eels for breakfast!"

Erica brushed a clump of brown hair out of her eyes. "Get over it, Wiglaf," she told him.

"I know, I know," Wiglaf said miserably. "The castle moat is swarming with eels. And as long as our headmaster can get eels for free, he will have Frypot cook us eels for breakfast, lunch, and dinner."

With her bread, Erica sopped up every last drop of dark green eel juice on her plate. She popped the bread into her mouth.

1

How could she stand it? Wiglaf wondered.

"Mmmm," Erica said. "I love it!"

Erica loved everything about DSA—including the eels. She didn't even mind emptying the eel traps each morning. Wiglaf was pretty sure that was one of the reasons she had won the Future Dragon Slayer of the Month Medal.

Wiglaf tasted a small bite of tail. Disgusting! He pushed his plate of eels across the table.

"Here, Erica," he said. "Have mine."

"Shhh! It's *Eric*, remember?" Erica looked around the dining hall to see whether anyone at the other tables had heard. "If Mordred discovers I'm a girl and kicks me out of school, it will be *your* fault!"

"Sorry," Wiglaf said.

"You're the only one who knows my secret," Erica went on. "If you tell anyone, I swear, I'll whack off your head! I'll plunge my sword into your gut! Your blood will—"

"All right, Eric!" Wiglaf cut in quickly. "I get your meaning."

Wiglaf knew Erica was dying to slay a dragon and become a hero. But did she have to go on and on about plunging her sword into *him*?

Wiglaf wanted to be a hero, too. Heroes were brave and bold. If he were a hero, no one would tease him about being small for his age. Or about his carrot-colored hair. So Wiglaf had left home, with his pet pig, Daisy, at his side. He had come to Dragon Slayers' Academy to learn how to kill dragons and become a hero.

There was only one small problem with his plan.

Wiglaf couldn't stand the sight of blood.

"Wiglaf! Eric!" someone called from across the dining hall.

Wiglaf looked up. He saw Angus, the headmaster's nephew, running toward their table.

Angus was plump and sandy-haired. He never ran when he could walk. He never walked when he could sit. So Wiglaf knew he must have important news.

"Angus!" Erica exclaimed. "What is it?"

Angus stood by the Class I table, catching his breath. "Uncle Mordred is having a tantrum," he said.

"That's nothing new," Wiglaf pointed out. Mordred was always yelling at him because of what had happened with a dragon named Gorzil. Wiglaf and Erica had been sent off to kill Gorzil. And Wiglaf *had* killed him. But only by accident. He had stumbled upon Gorzil's secret weakness—bad jokes. And four bad jokes later, Gorzil was history. But Mordred didn't yell about how he had killed the dragon. He yelled about how Wiglaf had let some greedy villagers take all of Gorzil's gold.

"But this is a major tantrum," Angus was saying. "Mordred just heard about a boy from Dragon Exterminators' Prep. He killed a dragon and brought his headmaster all the dragon's gold. Uncle Mordred is screaming and yelling that one of us had better slay a dragon soon.

One of us must bring him some gold, or—"

"Angus!" Wiglaf cried. "Duck!"

Angus ducked. A fat jellied eel flew over his head. It landed in Erica's lap.

Erica leaped to her feet. "Hey! Who threw that?" she called.

"Me!" yelled a boy from the Class II table. "What are you going to do about it?"

"You will see!" Erica yelled back. The Future Dragon Slayer of the Month loved a good food fight as much as any other DSA student. She snatched up an eel from Wiglaf's plate. She threw it. "Bull's-eye!" she yelled as it hit its mark.

At once the air was thick with flying eels.

Wiglaf grinned. Moments like this were the best part of being at Dragon Slayers' Academy! He grabbed an eel. He threw it across the room. Then he joined in the chant that boys at the Class III table had started: "No more eel! No more eel!"

Soon the dining hall was filled with the sound of feet stomping and voices chanting: "No more eel! No more eel!"

Wiglaf picked up the last eel from his plate. He eyed the life-sized bust of Mordred that sat on a post by the door. The headmaster's thick hair, his big popping eyes, and his wide smile had been carved into stone.

Wiglaf took aim. "This one is for you, Mordred!" he yelled. Then he hurled his eel at the stone head.

But at that very moment, the flesh-and-blood headmaster walked through the dining hall door.

Wiglaf stared in horror as his eel hit the real Mordred's face with a mighty splat!

Chapter 2

The eel stuck to Mordred's forehead. Green eel juice dripped into his angry violet eyes. It trickled down his cheeks to his beard.

"You!" Mordred roared at Wiglaf. "I should have known!" He ripped the flattened fish from his forehead. He threw it over his shoulder.

"You!" Mordred thundered. He glared at Wiglaf. "The only DSA pupil ever to slay a dragon! But did you bring me Gorzil's gold? You did NOT!"

"I-I tried to, sir," Wiglaf said. "But the villagers ran into Gorzil's cave, and—"

"Excuses! Excuses!" Mordred shouted. "And

you never paid your tuition! You still owe me seven pennies!"

"That is true," Wiglaf began. "But you see, sir, my family has no money. And my father wanted me to sell my pig. But I—"

"And now you go and hit me with an eel!" Mordred cut in. "As soon as you pay your seven pennies, I shall kick you out of school!"

Mordred took a big red handkerchief from his pocket. He wiped the last of the eel juice from his face.

"But, now," he continued, "it's detention for one and all!" He pointed a fat gold-ringed finger toward the stairs. "To the dungeon! March!"

The DSA students lined up. They marched down three flights of stone steps. One by one, the pupils filed into the cold, damp dungeon.

When everyone was inside, Mordred slammed the door. He lit a pair of torches on the wall.

"Angus! Come here!" the headmaster barked. "The rest of you, sit!"

Angus stepped forward. Wiglaf and the rest of the students sat down on the hard floor.

Mordred gave Angus a jar of quills and several bottles of ink. "Pass these around," he ordered. "Then give out the parchment."

Angus obeyed in silence.

At last everyone had writing supplies.

"Write down all one hundred rules for future dragon slayers," Mordred said. "Neatly, now. No cross-outs or ink blots allowed."

Erica's hand shot up. "Is there a prize for whoever finishes first?" she asked.

"No, Eric. This is a punishment." Mordred frowned at the hourglass he wore strapped to his wrist. "You have two hours. Begin!"

Two hours! Wiglaf's heart sank as he dipped his quill into an ink bottle. He wrote:

100 Rules for Future Dragon Slayers

1. A future dragon slayer will gladly lay

down his life to get gold for Mordred.
2. A future dragon slayer never
complains—especially in letters home.
3. A future dragon slayer eats what is on
his plate—no matter what it looks like.
4. Or tastes like.
5. Or smells like.

Five down, Wiglaf thought. Only ninety-five to go. He glanced over at Erica's paper. How had she written eighteen rules already?

6. A future dragon slayer must keep his
sword sharp and ready for action.

Swords! thought Wiglaf. *That's all anybody at DSA cares about.* He had killed a dragon! So what if he hadn't used his sword. He had done it with jokes. But shouldn't that count for something? It didn't seem to. Nobody seemed to think slaying a dragon with jokes was one bit heroic. Wiglaf sighed. How was he ever going to become a hero?

Wiglaf had just dipped his quill into the ink again when he heard a fluttering noise. He and several others looked up. At the barred window of the dungeon they saw the face of a giant bird!

Mordred looked up, too.

"Zounds!" he yelped. "A bird of evil omen has come to devour us all!"

"My lord!" the bird called. "It is I, your scout, Yorick." He reached out a wing tip and pulled off his big yellow beak. "See?"

"Yorick!" Mordred cried. "Quick! Come down here! Bring me your news!"

A moment later, Yorick waddled into the dungeon. He was covered from head to toe with grimy gray feathers.

"My lord," Yorick said, "I have been spying for you on Buzzard's Peak."

"Ah!" Mordred nodded. "So that explains your buzzard disguise."

Wiglaf thought Yorick looked like a huge pigeon. But he kept his thought to himself.

"My lord," Yorick went on, "a black cloud is blowing in from the east."

Mordred rolled his violet eyes. "I don't pay you to bring me weather reports, Yorick!"

"My lord," Yorick said, "this is no ordinary cloud. It is a cloud of smoke."

"Egad!" Mordred exclaimed. His eyes lit up with excitement. "You cannot mean..."

"I do, my lord," Yorick continued. "A dragon is headed this way. My sources say it is a she-dragon. She is hunting down the warrior who slew her son."

"*Oh!*" Mordred cried. "There is nothing more terrible than an angry mother dragon! I wonder who this unlucky warrior can be?" He tapped his gold-ringed fingers on his chin. "Sir Freddy Headwhacker? No, I'll bet it's that old rascal, Sir Percy Smackbottom."

"My lord," Yorick said, "they say it is the warrior who killed the dragon Gorzil."

"Gorzil?" Angus gasped. "Wiglaf! The dragon is coming after you!"

Chapter 3

Wiglaf suddenly had a bad feeling in his stomach. And it wasn't from the jellied eel.

"M-m-m-me?" he said.

"You, my boy!" Mordred exclaimed happily. "What luck!"

"Luck?" Wiglaf said. His heart pounded with fear. "It doesn't seem lucky to me."

At this moment, becoming a hero didn't seem so important. Staying alive—that's what mattered.

"Just think—a dragon coming right to my front door!" Mordred smiled. His gold front tooth shone in the torchlight. "Where there's a dragon, there are sure to be piles and piles of

GOLD close by! Oh, just thinking of it boggles the mind!"

"Sir?" Erica called out. "Remember how you sent Wiglaf and me out to kill Gorzil? Well, Wiglaf never even touched that dragon. He killed him by accident!"

"That's true, sir," Wiglaf added quickly.

"See?" Erica said. "Wiglaf even says it's true! But I was ready to kill Gorzil the right way! I had drawn my sword! I was ready to cut off Gorzil's ugly head! By all rights, it's me that Gorzil's mother should be hunting down!"

"Eric," Mordred said patiently, "who turned Gorzil into dragon dust?"

"Well, uh...Wiglaf," Erica admitted. "But—"

Mordred shook a finger at his student. "You must not be jealous of the feats of others," he scolded.

Erica slumped down. "Sorry, sir," she said.

"Are we clear on this?" Mordred asked. "The dragon is after Wiglaf? And Wiglaf alone?"

Wiglaf let out a groan.

"Yes, sir," Erica answered glumly.

"Good." Mordred turned back to his scout. "Yorick," he said, "when will the dragon be here?"

"My lord," Yorick replied, "I multiplied the length of the smoky cloud by its width. Then I subtracted the wind speed—"

"Spit it out, man!" Mordred yelled. "When?"

"My lord," Yorick said, "when the noon bell rings on Friday, Seetha will arrive."

"Friday!" Wiglaf cried. "But that's only two days from—"

"Hush!" Mordred clamped a hand over Wiglaf's mouth. "Yorick! What did you say the dragon's name was?"

"Seetha, my lord," said Yorick.

The smile faded from Mordred's face. "Seetha? The Beast from the East? No!" he wailed. "It can't be! This is too, too horrible!"

Wiglaf started shaking. Seetha must be awful indeed to make Mordred act this way!

"Yorick!" Mordred cried. "I beg you! Say her name is Deetha! Or Queetha! Or Loreetha!"

Yorick only shook his head.

"No dragon has ever come to DSA!" Mordred exclaimed. "Now one is coming. Any dragon in the world would bring along its golden hoard. Any dragon but one. And that one is Seetha!"

"She has no gold?" Angus asked.

"No!" Mordred cried. Tears sprang to his violet eyes. "Seetha cares nothing for gold! All she cares about is killing. She does it for fun!"

"For fun?" Wiglaf squeaked. He started shaking harder. And his teeth began to chatter. "But what does she...How does she..."

"Oh, Seetha loves fun and games," Mordred said. "She plays with her victims for hours before she makes her kill. But she has no gold!" he moaned. "Woe is me! No gold!"

He waved a hand toward the dungeon door. "Go, boys. Detention is over. Just go. Leave me to my sorrow!"

Erica jumped to her feet. "Sir!" she cried. "What you need is a DSA cheer!" She turned to the rest of the students. "Let's do *Look Out, Dragons!* Really yell it now. Ready? And!"

Then everyone—everyone but Wiglaf— marched out of the dungeon shouting:

> *"Look out, dragons! Here we come!*
> *DSA! That's where we're from!*
> *Will we slay you?*
> *Yes! We will!*
> *Here we come to kill! Kill! Kill!"*

Chapter 4

"**G**orzil's mother is coming to get me!" Wiglaf moaned. He lay on his cot that afternoon during rest hour. "Oh, I'm toast!"

"Pipe down, Wiglaf!" said a tall boy in a cot by the door. "Some of us are trying to rest."

"Go blow your nose, Torblad!" Erica snapped. She sat on the edge of Wiglaf's cot. "I hate to think what you would be like if a dragon was hunting you down!"

Wiglaf moaned louder. He turned to a picture he had drawn of his pig, Daisy, curled up in her cozy bed in the DSA henhouse.

"My poor Daisy!" Wiglaf said. "When I'm gone, she will be all alone in the world."

"That's the least of your worries," Angus offered from his cot on the other side of

Wiglaf's. "Here. This will make you feel better." He broke off a piece of his Camelot Crunch Bar. He handed it to Wiglaf. "Maybe you should run away before Seetha gets here," he added. "Maybe you should go home."

"I can't." Wiglaf passed the candy on to Erica. He was not hungry. "My father told me not to come home without a pile of gold. And he has a temper as bad as Mordred's."

"Uncle Mordred isn't so tough," Angus said. "You should see him when my Aunt Lobelia comes for a visit. She is his big sister. And boy, does she ever boss him around. Once—"

"Angus! Stop talking about your aunt!" Erica broke in. "We have to help Wiggie figure out how he's going to kill Seetha. Look."

Erica reached into her pocket. She brought out two small lead figures. One was a tiny Sir Lancelot. The other was a tiny dragon.

"Here is how *The Sir Lancelot Handbook* says to do it," she said. "'Take up your sword. Smite the dragon on the noggin!'"

Erica made the little Lancelot bonk the little dragon three times on the head.

"*Arrrrgh!*" she wailed. She made the little dragon flop down on its side. "I'm done for!"

"But Seetha won't hold still while I try to smite her!" Wiglaf said. "And let's face it," he added, "I'm no Sir Lancelot."

"I'll say," Erica snorted.

"What you need to do," Angus said, "is find out Seetha's secret weakness. If you can do that, you won't have to smite her."

"I was lucky to have guessed Gorzil's weakness," Wiglaf said. "But what are the chances of that happening again?"

"You don't need luck," Angus said. "You need the right book. There are loads of dragon books in the DSA library."

"What?" Erica exclaimed. "DSA has a library?"

"We have a free period after rest hour," Wiglaf said. "Let's hit the library!"

Chapter 5

BONG! The bell ending rest hour rang.

Angus led Wiglaf and Erica out to the castle yard. Afternoon classes had just begun.

Sir Mort's Stalking Class was learning how to sneak up on a dragon from behind.

Coach Plungett was teaching his Slaying Class the Gut Stab on the practice dragon.

The boys in Frypot's Scrubbing Class were down on their hands and knees washing the castle steps. Mordred claimed that scrubbing was an important skill for future dragon slayers. But Wiglaf never understood exactly why.

The three reached the South Tower. They

ran up a winding stone staircase to the DSA library.

Brother Dave, the librarian, looked up as they walked in. He had a round face and small, round glasses. He wore a brown monk's robe.

"Good day, Angus!" Brother Dave exclaimed. "I see thou hast brought some friends here with thee on this fine afternoon!"

Brother Dave's order of monks had to do good deeds. The deeds had to be so hard that most people could never do them. Brother Dave had decided to become the librarian at DSA, where few of the students—and none of the teachers—had ever read a whole book.

"Art thou here to work on a report that shall keep thee in the library many hours?" Brother Dave asked. He looked hopeful.

"No," Wiglaf replied. "I'm not here about school work...."

"Oh! A child who reads for pleasure!" Brother Dave clasped his hands to his heart. He looked thrilled. "Maybe thou would like

The King Who Couldn't Sleep by Eliza Wake. A great story. Or perhaps thou might try *Into the Dark Forest* by Hugo First. Or, if thou likes poetry—"

"Brother Dave?" Angus cut in. "My friend Wiglaf here is in trouble. He is going to be roasted in two days unless we can get some facts about the dragon Seetha."

"Seetha?" Brother Dave gasped. "Canst thou mean the Beast from the East?"

"You've heard of her, too?" Wiglaf cried. "Oh, please, Brother Dave! I need a book that will tell me Seetha's secret weakness!"

Brother Dave grew thoughtful. "I know of only one book that might tell thee that," he said. "Let me get it." He dashed off and returned with *The Encyclopedia of Dragons*.

Wiglaf gladly took the big book from the monk. Here in his very hands he might be holding the key to Seetha's downfall. Who knew? Perhaps he would live to see Saturday after all!

Wiglaf turned the pages to the "S" section. He kept turning. At last he saw the name *Seetha*. A hideous face stared back at him from the page.

"Whoa!" Angus exclaimed. "That is one scary dragon lady!"

A horn grew out of Seetha's head. Pink curly tentacles sprouted from the base of the horn. They hung down over her yellow eyes. A long tongue curved out of her fang-filled mouth.

"She looks mean, all right," Erica said. "Where do you think you will plunge your sword, Wiggie? Here, in Seetha's neck? Or in her heart? Or maybe in her big, fat gut? Or—"

"Stop!" Wiglaf said. "Let us see what the book has to say."

What it had to say was this:

Full name: *Seetha von Flambé*
Also known as: *The Beast from the East*
Husband: *Fangol von Flambé*
(slain by Sir Gristle McThistle in 1143 A.D.)

Children: 3,684

Appearance:

    Scales: swamp green

    Horn: burnt orange

    Eyes: yes

    Teeth: disgusting!

Age: one thousand and counting

Most often heard saying:

    "Let's go torch a wizard's tower!"

Best known for:

    smelling bad...really, REALLY bad

Biggest surprise:

    she's not into gold

Hobby: playing fun killing games

Favorite thing in all the world:

    Son #92, Gorzil, her darling boy

"Oh, I'm doomed!" cried Wiglaf.

"This does not look good for you, Wiggie," Erica said.

The three friends read on. Wiglaf turned the page. Suddenly they all gasped. At the top of the page, it said:

Secret weakness:

Knights who know say Seetha's fatal weakness is ba—

Ink had spilled over the page. The rest of the word was covered with a thick black blob.

"Ba— what?" Wiglaf cried. "I need to know!"

Angus held the page up to the burning candle on Brother Dave's desk. "I can't make out the rest of the word," he said. "But maybe Seetha's weakness is the same as Gorzil's—bad jokes."

Erica shook her head. "No two dragons have the same secret weakness," she said. "I read that in *The Sir Lancelot Handbook*."

"But ba— could be so many things," Angus pointed out. "Bananas. Ballads. Barbecued beef on a bun."

"Looks like you are going to have to slay this dragon the old-fashioned way—with your sword," Erica told Wiglaf. "If I were you, I'd ask Coach Plungett for some extra help in slashing and bashing."

Wiglaf nearly gagged at the thought. "But I'm no good at that stuff!"

"If I were thee," the monk said, gazing down at Wiglaf, "I would start saying my prayers!"

Chapter 6

"Ba— could be bait," Angus said. "Or balloons. Or—"

"We have to go," Erica cut in. "Or we'll be late for Slaying. Thanks, Brother Dave!"

"Ba— could be banjos or back rubs or badminton," Angus went on as they left the library.

"I'm doomed!" Wiglaf exclaimed. "Doomed!"

"Stop being so gloomy!" Erica ordered. "Even if the worst happens, death by dragon is a noble way to die."

"But I don't want to die!" Wiglaf cried.

"Ba— could be baskets," Angus kept on as they ran down the steps. "Or baboons. Or battle-axes."

"It could be a thousand different things," Wiglaf said. "Oh, I wish I could just disappear!"

Angus stopped suddenly.

"Keep moving!" Erica said.

"Disappear," Angus said. He began walking slowly down the steps again. "That gives me an idea. Maybe my Aunt Lobelia could help you, Wiglaf. For there are those who say"— he dropped his voice— "that Lobelia is a sorceress."

"Do *you* think she is?" Wiglaf asked.

Angus nodded. "My mother is always saying that Lobelia can transform people. That she works wonders on them. And you know what?" He smiled. "Mordred keeps a room for Lobelia here in the castle."

Wiglaf stopped dead in his tracks.

"Move!" Erica cried. "You don't want to be late, do you?"

But Wiglaf didn't move. "Angus, do you think Lobelia has something in her room that might transform me?" he asked. "Something to make me disappear for a few days?"

"She might." Angus grinned. "Let's go see. I happen to know that Uncle Mordred keeps the key to her room on a nail over his desk."

"Sneaking in is against DSA rules," Erica reminded them. She fingered her Future Dragon Slayer of the Month Medal which she wore on a ribbon around her neck. "But don't worry," she added. "If you two go, I won't tell. Now, out of my way. I'm going to Slaying." Erica pushed past Wiglaf and Angus. She hurried down the stairs.

Ten minutes later, Angus lifted the latch and slowly opened Mordred's office door. He peeked inside.

"All clear," he whispered.

Wiglaf walked into the office behind Angus. He didn't want to think what the headmaster would do to them if he caught them there.

The boys made their way to the key. They had just reached it when a low moan startled them.

Wiglaf turned. Yikes! There was Mordred! Angus hadn't seen him because he was lying down on his velvet couch.

Mordred had put on a pair of red pajamas. Tears rolled down his cheeks. He was mumbling to himself, "A dragon with no gold. Alas! The thought of it makes me ill!"

Wiglaf sighed with relief. Mordred was suffering far too much to notice them.

Angus lifted the key silently off its nail. Then the boys left the office.

In the hallway, Angus burst out laughing. "What a baby Mordred is!" he exclaimed. "Say, maybe that's Seetha's weakness— babies!"

"Give it up, Angus," Wiglaf said. "We will

never guess Seetha's weakness. I'm pinning my hopes on Aunt Lobelia."

Wiglaf and Angus hurried through dark hallways. At last they came to a wide door in the East Tower. Angus put the key in the lock. *Click!* The door opened.

Wiglaf stepped inside. It was very dark. He swallowed. Maybe breaking into a sorceress's room was not such a good idea. What if it was booby-trapped? What if Lobelia had cast spells against trespassers?

Angus felt his way over to the curtains. He pushed them back. Light flooded in.

Wiglaf looked around. He had expected to see shelves packed with jars of nettles and toadstools. He had very much hoped to see bottles labeled "Invisibility Potion" or "Dragon Repellent."

But instead he saw a fancy sitting room. Dozens of large trunks were lined up against the walls. In the far corner stood a three-sided mirror. Tapestries hung on the walls. Each one showed St. George in some bloody stage of killing a dragon. Wiglaf looked away. Even blood stitched into a tapestry made him sick.

"Maybe she keeps her potions in the trunks." Angus bent down to check one. "It's open," he whispered.

As Wiglaf helped him raise the lid, a husky voice called from the doorway: "Freeze!"

Wiglaf and Angus froze.

"Step away from the trunk," the voice went on. "And I mean *now*!"

Chapter 7

"Turn around, you little snoops," the voice said. "Let me have a look at you."

Wiglaf shook with fear as he turned.

"Aunt Lobelia!" Angus exclaimed.

"Angus?" The woman gasped. She dropped her traveling bags. "My stars!"

"I didn't know you were coming for a visit, Auntie," Angus said.

"That's pretty obvious," Lobelia told him.

Wiglaf saw that Angus's Aunt Lobelia had the same thick dark hair as Mordred. She had the same violet eyes, too. But the headmaster was stout. And Lobelia was as thin as a rail.

The sorceress did not look happy. Wiglaf swallowed. What if she turned him into a toad?

A pair of lean hounds with jeweled collars stood at Lobelia's side. The dogs began barking as they, too, recognized Angus.

"Shush, Demon! Lucifer, stop it!" Lobelia said. She threw off a blue velvet cape. Under it, she wore a silvery gown. "So, what are you two after? My jewels?"

"No, Auntie," Angus said. "I'm sorry we broke in. But it's an emergency. This is my friend Wiglaf. He needs help. The dragon Seetha is coming after him!"

"Seetha?" Lobelia cried. "The Beast from the East?"

Wiglaf nodded.

"So it's you she is after! But why?"

"Well, I...um, sort of...by accident, killed her son," Wiglaf explained.

"Bad move," Lobelia said. "On my way here, I passed through the village of Wormbelly. Seetha had just been there. And she left behind her horrible stink." Lobelia wrinkled her nose. "Someone should give that dragon a bottle of perfume. Anyway," she continued, "it seems that Seetha made a mistake. She thought the biggest, strongest man in Wormbelly killed her son. Oh, how she tortured the poor man! She made him play 'Ring Around the Rosie' until he fell down and could not get up."

"Say no more, I beg of you!" Wiglaf cried.

Lobelia shook her head. "Some villagers think he may get his wits back one day. But others fear the worst."

Wiglaf let out a little squeak.

"Seetha will be here at noon on Friday," Angus said. "Can you help Wiglaf, Auntie?"

"Of course I can help," Lobelia answered.

Wiglaf dropped to his knees. "Oh, thank you, Lady Lobelia!" Yes! A sorceress was going to use her magic to help him! Why, he was as good as saved. He grabbed Lobelia's hand and tried to kiss it.

Lobelia yanked her hand away. "Get up!" she ordered. Then she began circling Wiglaf.

She tilted her head. She looked at him from every which way.

"For starters," she said at last, "I'd lose the DSA tunic. And those old breeches. A leather tunic would be nice for you. Brown, to bring out the carrot color of your hair."

Wiglaf had never seen a sorceress at work before. But this was not what he had expected.

Lobelia walked over to her trunks. She started throwing open the lids. From one trunk, she pulled a shirt with billowing sleeves and a pair of quilted yellow breeches. From another, she took brown boots. From still another, forest green leggings and a helmet.

"The ram's horns on this helmet make a strong statement. Don't you think so?" Lobelia asked. "Oh! And this wolf pelt! It's perfect! You can drape it over one shoulder for a sort of Viking effect."

Lobelia piled the clothing into Wiglaf's arms. "Go behind that tapestry and change. We won't peek," she told him. "You know,

Wiglaf, clothes make the man. Or, in your case, the boy. Go on, now! Hurry!"

Wiglaf gave Angus a puzzled look. But he did as he was told. After all, who was he to question the ways of a sorceress?

Wiglaf took off his DSA tunic and his breeches. He put on the shirt. Then he pulled on the green leggings and the heavy yellow breeches. He slipped the leather tunic on over his head. He put on the boots and draped the wolf pelt over his shoulder, Viking style. Finally, he put the ram's-horn helmet on his head. He felt like a fool as he stepped out from behind the tapestry.

Demon and Lucifer began to growl at him.

Angus giggled—until a sharp look from Lobelia made him stop.

"Turn around, Wiglaf," Lobelia ordered. "Let me see the new you!"

Wiglaf turned.

"I am a genius!" Lobelia clapped her hands.

"Seetha will drop *dead* when she sees you!"

"She will?" Wiglaf exclaimed. "For sure?"

"Well, in a manner of speaking," Lobelia answered.

Wiglaf's heart sank. "I didn't think it could be that easy," he said. "But, Lady Lobelia! I need Seetha *really* and *truly* to drop dead! Or she will kill me! Oh, I know you have the power to help me! Angus said—" Wiglaf stopped. He shot a look at his friend.

"Said what?" Lobelia asked. She turned to her nephew. "Angus? Speak up!"

"I said..." Angus mumbled. "I said...uh...that you might be a sorceress."

"A sorceress!" Lobelia's eyes flashed with anger. "Who told you such a thing?"

"My mother," Angus answered.

"What? My own sister?" Lobelia cried.

Angus nodded. "She said that you could transform people. That you worked wonders."

"Oh, now I see." Lobelia smiled. "That part is true enough. I *do* transform people. Have you ever heard of King Richard the Lion-Hearted?"

Wiglaf and Angus nodded.

"Before I fixed him up, you know what people called him?" Lobelia asked. "Chicken-Hearted Richie, that's what! Who do you think put him in the bold red tunic? Who do you think told him to blacken his beard? Me!" Lobelia exclaimed. "Me!

"I transformed that man," she went on. "And I have transformed you, Wiglaf. Listen, if Seetha sees you as a little DSA student, she'll fry you! And from what I hear, she'll take her own sweet time about it, too."

Wiglaf swallowed.

"But," Lobelia went on, "if Seetha sees you as a mighty hero, she'll respect you. And who knows? Maybe she won't even kill you."

"That would be good," Wiglaf said. "Thank you, Lady Lobelia."

Lobelia smiled. "Dress like a hero, Wiglaf, and you *are* a hero. That's my motto!"

Chapter 8

"Sorry, Wiglaf," Angus said as he and Wiglaf left Lobelia's room.

"Me, too," Wiglaf said. He straightened his ram's-horn helmet. It was so heavy! And the wolf pelt made his neck itch. Worst of all, he didn't believe that the silly clothes would scare Seetha. He wished he had thought to get his clothes back from Lobelia. What would the other boys say when they saw him?

They reached Mordred's office. Angus opened the door and entered the room.

Wiglaf peeked in. He saw that Mordred had fallen asleep.

Angus reached up to put the key back.

But as he did, Mordred's eyes popped open.

"Angus?" he said. "What are you up to?" Then he saw Wiglaf at the door.

"Blazing King Ken's britches!" he yelled. He sat up. "What are *you* supposed to be?"

Wiglaf stepped into the headmaster's office. "It's...er, a hero look, sir," he said.

"To scare off Seetha," Angus added.

"Bite your tongue, nephew!" Mordred exclaimed. "And never say the name of that no-good, no-gold dragon around me again!"

Mordred mopped his face with his big red hanky. He turned back to Wiglaf. "Where on earth did you ever get such a silly outfit?"

"Lady Lobelia gave me the clothes, sir," Wiglaf answered.

"Oh, Lobelia. That explains it." Mordred nodded. Then his eyes widened in horror. "Egad!" he cried. "Lobelia's *here*?"

"Yes, Uncle," Angus said.

"She never sent word that she was coming," Mordred complained. "I don't suppose she said how long she plans to stay."

Angus shook his head.

"Oh, I'm at death's door already! Five minutes with Lobelia will finish me off!" Mordred exclaimed. "Shoo, boys! Be off! Be gone! Leave me to enjoy what little peace I have left!"

Wiglaf backed away from the miserable headmaster. As he did, he saw a newspaper on Mordred's desk. The headline made Wiglaf's eyes widen in horror.

Wiglaf's hand shook as he picked up *The Medieval Times*. Angus looked over his shoulder. Together they read:

DRAGON LADY HUNTS SLAYER OF SON
Gorzil, Son #92, Was Mama's Darling Boy

RATSWHISKERS, Sept. 32nd
The dragon Seetha von Flambé, also known as the Beast from the East, is fighting mad. She and her late husband, Fangol, had some 3,684 young dragons. But one little dragon stood out from the others, and that was Gorzil.

"Gorzil was special," his mother told reporters just before she set fire to East Ratswhiskers yesterday. "When I find the brute who killed him, I don't know what I'll do. But it won't be pretty!"

Lifetime winner of the Stinkiest Dragon Award, Seetha is known as a fun-loving gal. She likes playing games. But when she plays games with her victims, Seetha has all the fun. She brought down Sir Featherbrain by making him do the hokeypokey until he could no longer put his left foot in. She has snuffed out the lives of other brave knights in ways too horrible to mention.

To the warrior who killed Seetha's darling boy, we can only say...Bye-bye!

Wiglaf gulped. He was more scared than he had ever been in his life. Now he almost wished Lobelia had turned him into a toad. At least he would be alive!

Chapter 9

Wiglaf didn't sleep a wink that night. On Thursday morning, he got up, thinking, *This could be the last day of my life!*

Well, he'd do his best to make it a good one.

Wiglaf put on his hero outfit and stuck his sword in his belt. He went to breakfast and ate some scrambled eel. Then he headed for Dragon Science Class with his friends.

"Ba— could be bats," Angus told Wiglaf as they walked. "Vampire bats are pretty scary."

"Maybe it's bandits," Erica put in.

"But Seetha has no gold for bandits to take," Angus said. "Hey! Maybe it's baked beans."

Wiglaf scratched his neck. The mangy wolf

pelt was giving him a nasty rash. He was hard-ly even listening to Angus and Erica who went on and on about every ba— word under the sun. He knew his friends were only trying to help. But what was the use? Guessing Seetha's secret weakness was impossible!

The three walked into science class.

"Looky! Looky!" Torblad yelled. "Here comes Mr. Puffy Pants!"

Wiglaf tried to look as if he didn't care. All day yesterday, boys had teased him. They said the wolf pelt looked like road kill. They said his helmet had cow horns on it. Every time he went by, they yelled out, *"Moooo!"* But Mr. Puffy Pants. That was even worse!

So much for having a good day.

"Button it up, Torblad!" Erica yelled back. "You *wish* you had puffy pants like Wiglaf's!"

The Dragon Science teacher, tall, thin Dr. Pluck, stood at the front of the room.

"**P**lease sto**p, pup**ils!" Dr. Pluck sputtered.

Dr. Pluck's lips were badly chapped because

he always spit when he said the letter *p*. DSA students made sure they came to Dr. Pluck's class early. They all wanted to get seats in the back rows to keep from getting sprayed.

Wiglaf, Erica, and Angus had not come early. So they took the only empty seats—in the first row.

"**P**lease **p**ay attention, **pup**ils," Dr. Pluck sputtered. He pulled down a large chart of a dragon. All its body parts were labeled. Dr. Pluck put his pointer on the dragon's belly. "The **plum**p **p**art here is the **p**aunch," he told the class. "Its scientific name is the **pipp**i-hi**pp**o-**papp**a-**pee**pus."

Erica's hand shot up. "Can you spell that for us, sir?"

"With **p**leasure," said Dr. Pluck. "**P**-i-**p**-**p**-"

Wiglaf didn't care about spelling right then. He didn't care about parts of a dragon. He didn't even care that Dr. Pluck was spraying him with spit. He stared at the dragon chart.

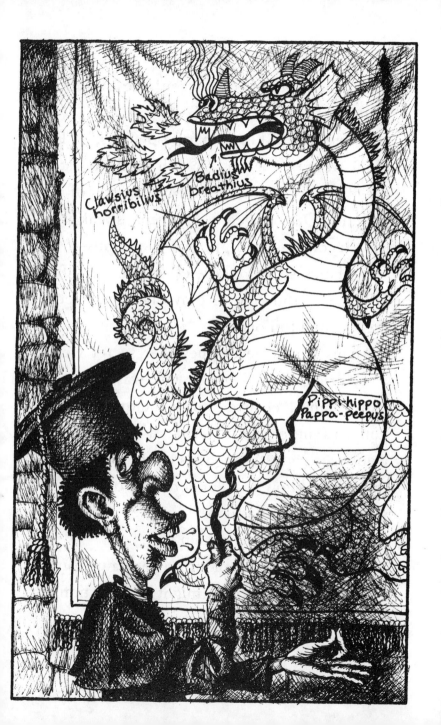

But all he could see was the face of Seetha from Brother Dave's book.

"The **pipp**i-hi**pp**o-**papp**a-**pee**pus," Dr. Pluck went on, "is **p**acked with **p**artly digested **p**ieces of food. **P**ossibly **p**art of a **p**ossum. Or a **p**igeon. **P**lunge a s**p**ear into the dragon's **pipp**i-hi**pp**o-**papp**a-**pee**pus—"

Dr. Pluck showered the class with facts. But Wiglaf was thinking of only one fact. Seetha was coming tomorrow!

Angus would never guess her secret weakness. Erica talked big. But talk was easy. She didn't stand a chance against the dragon. And Lobelia's hero outfit? What a joke! Seetha would see right through his clothes. And then she would know that, under the wolf pelt, he was anything but a hero.

Was there no one to help him?

"In a dragon's **pipp**i-hi**pp**o-**papp**a-**pee**pus," Dr. Pluck was spraying, "might be a **p**ortion of a **p**ig or a—"

Wiglaf suddenly heard Dr. Pluck's words. Pig. Pig. PIG! Yes! Daisy might help him! True, she was a pig. But she was wiser than most people he knew. And, ever since the wizard Zelnoc had put a spell on her, Daisy could speak Pig Latin. Maybe she could tell him how to save himself. Even if she couldn't, Wiglaf wanted to see her. One last time.

So, after Dragon Science, Wiglaf cut Scrubbing. He headed for the henhouse.

"Daisy?" Wiglaf called softly. He didn't want to bother the hens. "Where are you?"

Wiglaf heard the patter of feet on the dirt floor. His pig dashed from her bed. She let out a scream.

Hens fluttered and squawked.

"It's me, Daisy!" Wiglaf exclaimed.

"Iglaf-Way?" Daisy said, backing up.

"Of course it's me." Wiglaf took off the ram's-horn helmet. "See?"

Once Daisy and the hens got used to his

hero look, Wiglaf sat down with his pig. Daisy snuggled up to Wiglaf and listened as he told her about Gorzil's mother.

"Eetha-Say?" Daisy gasped. "E-thay east-bay om-fray e-thay east-yay?"

"Yes. The Beast from the East." Wiglaf nodded sadly. "Her secret weakness begins with ba—. But that is all I know."

In a shaky voice Daisy said, "Acon-bay?"

"Maybe bacon *is* her weakness," Wiglaf said. "But I will never let Seetha get you, Daisy!" He planted a kiss on her snout. "The dragon will be here at noon tomorrow. What shall I do?"

"All-cay Elnoc-Zay," the pig answered.

"The wizard?" Wiglaf said. "But Zelnoc's spells always turn out wrong. He said so himself. He was in for repairs when we met him."

"En-thay oo-whay?" Daisy asked.

"Who, indeed?" Wiglaf thought for a while. "All right, Daisy," he said at last. "I shall call Zelnoc. For even a broken wizard is better than no wizard at all."

Chapter 10

In those days, everyone knew how to call a wizard. All Wiglaf had to do was say Zelnoc's name backwards three times.

Wiglaf wrote on the dirt floor of the henhouse with his finger: Z E L N O C.

Then he wrote it backwards: C O N L E Z.

"Conlez, Conlez, Conlez," Wiglaf chanted.

Suddenly, a tiny bit of smoke appeared. It grew into a smoky, blue pillar. Out of the smoke stepped Zelnoc. He had on a pointed hat and a blue robe covered with stars.

"Bats and blisters!" Zelnoc yelled. "Am I called to a henhouse?" He turned to Wiglaf. "Who are you? Wait! Don't tell me. It's coming to me now. You tried to pull me out of Wizards' Bog. It's Wigwam, right?"

"Wiglaf, sir. Thank you for coming."

"You think I had a choice?" Zelnoc shook his head. "No such thing. When we wizards are called, we show up. Have to. It's Wizard Rule #598."

Now Daisy spoke. "Ello-hay, izard-way."

"Hello, pig! Where in the world did you learn to speak Pig Latin? Oh, I remember. My spell went wrong." Zelnoc sighed. "My spells always do. Well, what can I do for you, Wiglump? Tell me quickly! I want to get back to the Wizards' Convention. Zizmor the Amazing was just starting a demonstration. Oh, what that wizard can do with a few newts' eyes and a drop of bat's blood! And you should see his new wizard's staff. It's a ten-speed model! It casts any spell in half the time."

"I could use a fast spell," Wiglaf said. "For tomorrow, the dragon Seetha is coming to kill me."

"Seetha?" Zelnoc drew back from Wiglaf. "The Pest from the West?"

"No," said Wiglaf. "The Beast from the East."

"Humph," Zelnoc said. "Never heard of that one."

"Well, she's coming to get me," Wiglaf told the wizard. "I'm scared to death! That's why I called you. Can you cast a spell to help me?"

Zelnoc scratched his ear. "A courage spell would fix you up. But can I remember one?"

Zelnoc thought for a minute. Then he snapped his fingers. "Got it! Quick, Wigloaf! Let me say it over you before I forget."

Zelnoc pushed up his sleeves. He stretched out his arms toward Wiglaf. He waggled his fingers.

"Just loosening myself up a bit," the wizard said. "All right. Count to three for me, pig."

"One-yay," said Daisy. "Oo-tway. Ee-thray!"

Zelnoc began to chant:

"Roses are red.

Violets are blue.

Sugar is—"

"Excuse me, sir?" Wiglaf broke in.

"Never stop a wizard midspell!" Zelnoc yelled. "Never!"

"But are you sure that's how a *courage* spell starts?" Wiglaf asked.

Zelnoc thought for a moment. "It doesn't sound right, does it?" He tapped his head with his finger. "Oh, courage spell? Where are you? Ah! There you are! Count again, pig!"

Daisy did: "One-yay. Oo-tway. Ee-thray!"

Zelnoc put one hand on his hip. He bent his other arm and stuck it out to the side. Then he began to sing:

"I'm a little teapot, short and stout!

Here is my handle! Here is my spout!"

"Op-stay, izard-way!" Daisy yelled.

"Sir!" Wiglaf cried. "That can not be it either!"

"Oh, toads and warts!" Zelnoc exclaimed. "I'll call Zizmor. He'll get it right."

Zelnoc shut his eyes and chanted: "*Romziz, Romziz, Romziz!*"

Nothing happened.

He tried again. "*Romziz, Romziz, Romziz!*"

Again, nothing happened.

"Slugs and leeches!" Zelnoc roared. He threw his pointed hat to the ground. He began jumping up and down on it, shouting over and over, "*Romziz! Romziz! Romziz!*"

POOF! Smoke filled the henhouse. Red smoke. Yellow smoke. Bright purple smoke.

The hens sprang from their nests. They raced out of the henhouse, clucking loudly.

"Un-ray, Iglaf-Way!" Daisy yelled.

But Wiglaf stood where he was. He watched in amazement as the smoke swirled into great columns. Out of each column stepped a wizard wearing a gown the color of the smoke. Some two dozen wizards appeared in all. They looked around, muttering.

"Zelnoc?" Wiglaf whispered. "Are these friends of yours?"

"Oh, my stars!" Zelnoc exclaimed. "I've called the whole convention!"

A very tall red-robed wizard with bright red eyes pounded his staff on the floor. The other wizards quieted.

"Did you call me?" the red wizard asked Wiglaf.

"Why...no, sir," Wiglaf said. "You see, Zelnoc thought—"

"Zelnoc!" The red wizard whirled around. "You! I should have known!"

"Sorry, Amazing One," Zelnoc said. He picked up his crumpled hat and stuck it on his head. "I only meant to call you, Ziz. Just you."

Zizmor the Amazing snorted. "Well, what did you want?"

"Tomorrow, this poor boy must fight Seetha," Zelnoc said. He pushed Wiglaf forward.

"Seetha?" Zizmor gasped. "The Beast from the East?"

"Yes, sir," Wiglaf answered.

The lesser wizards whispered darkly among themselves: "Oh, he's a goner. Poor boy. Doesn't stand a chance."

"So," Zelnoc continued, "I said to myself, 'Zelnoc, old sock, old bean, who better to cast a courage spell on this poor lad than Zizmor the Amazing?'"

Zizmor raised an eyebrow. "As it happens, I have been working on a new courage spell. But it's still in the experimental stage."

"I'll try anything!" Wiglaf said. "Please, sir! Can you help me?"

"Does a troll live under a bridge?" Zizmor answered. "Of course I can. And I shall. With pleasure. I would dearly love to take revenge on that fire-breathing beast myself."

"Why is that, sir?" Wiglaf asked.

"Seetha burned down my tower," Zizmor

said. "For no reason. Just flew over, leaned down, and torched it." The Amazing One shook his head. "It's been nothing but carpenters, painters, plumbers, and stonemasons ever since. I hate to think what the final bill is going to be." He closed his red eyes. He breathed deeply to calm himself.

"All right, my boy," Zizmor said, opening his eyes once more. "Are you ready for a dose of courage?"

"I think so, sir," Wiglaf answered.

"I shall give you a double dose," Zizmor said. "No, for Seetha, triple, I think. My triple spell doesn't last too long. But while it's working it's a zinger!"

"Ood-gay uck-lay Iglaf-Way!" Daisy whispered.

Wiglaf waved to his pig. Then he crossed his fingers for luck and got ready for the spell.

Zizmor the Amazing called his fellow wizards to make a circle around Wiglaf. They all stretched out their arms toward him. Zizmor held his ten-speed staff over Wiglaf's head. In a low voice, he chanted:

> *"Spineless, gutless, weak-kneed brat,*
> *Chicken-hearted scaredy-cat,*
> *Cringing coward, yellow-belly,*
> *Lily-livered, heart of jelly.*
> *Change this boy who's standing here,*
> *Into He-Who-Knows-No-Fear!"*

Sparks began to fly from Zizmor's staff.

Wiglaf gasped as they showered down on him. *Ziz! Ziz! Ziz!* The sparks flashed and popped. The roar of rushing wind filled Wiglaf's ears. And then the wizards began to swirl before his eyes.

The next thing Wiglaf knew, he was lying on the henhouse floor.

All the wizards stared down at him.

Zelnoc's face appeared close to Wiglaf's. "Speak to me, lad!" he cried. "Speak to me!"

Chapter 11

"Where is Seetha?" Wiglaf growled. He leaped to his feet. "Where is that ugly dragon?"

"Uh—thought you said she was coming tomorrow," Zelnoc said.

"I can't wait until tomorrow!" Wiglaf exclaimed.

He snatched his ram's-horn helmet from the floor. He jammed it on his head. "I shall save the world from the Beast from the East today! First, I shall slash Seetha's throat!" He drew his sword and sliced at the air. "Then I shall stab her through the heart!" He lunged forward, shouting, "Take *that*, you scaly scavenger!"

"Oh, dear," Zelnoc said. "Maybe the triple spell was a little much, Ziz."

"Fiddlesticks," Zizmor scoffed. "All right, fellow enchanters!" he called to the other wizards. "Clearly our work here is finished. Let's get back to the convention, shall we? I believe there's a brew-tasting party tonight."

"Wait for me, Ziz!" Zelnoc said. "Good luck, Wigloop!"

"Luck? Who needs luck?" Wiglaf exclaimed. "Not I! For I have courage!"

"Oh, dear," Zelnoc said again as smoke began to fill the henhouse.

Ten seconds later, both the smoke and the wizards had disappeared.

Wiglaf charged out of the henhouse. He waved his sword and shouted:

"Look out, Seetha! Here I come!
DSA ! That's where I'm from!
Will I slay you?
Yes! I will!
Here I come to kill! Kill! Kill!"

Daisy ran to the henhouse door. She called after him, "Ait-way, Iglaf-Way!"

"Sorry, pork chop," Wiglaf called back. "I have a dragon to slay!"

He-Who-Knows-No-Fear marched across the castle yard. From the tips of the ram's horns on his helmet down to the toes of his new boots, every inch of him was filled with courage. There was only one thing he wanted—action!

"Seetha's a fun-loving dragon, is she?" Wiglaf growled. "Well! Let's see how much fun she has when I stab her in the pippi-hippo-pappa-peepus!"

Wiglaf saw that Sir Mort had brought the Class I students out to the castle steps. They were having a Rubbish Relay. This was a scheme of Mordred's for getting the litter in the castle yard picked up.

"Wiglaf!" Erica called. "We were looking for you!" She and Angus broke away from the group. They ran up to him.

Angus waved a piece of parchment. "I've started a ba— list. I'll find Seetha's weakness yet! Listen—bald men, ballet dancers, bank robbers, barbers, baton twirlers, barking dogs—"

"Stop!" Wiglaf yelled. "What care I for Seetha's weakness? I shall slay her with my sword!"

Erica's eyes grew wide. "Wiglaf! You don't sound like yourself. Where are you going, anyway?"

"I am off to find the Beast from the East!" Wiglaf exclaimed. "I'll not wait for her to hunt me down. Nay! I shall hunt *her* down! I shall cut that dragon into a thousand pieces!"

"All *right*, Wiggie!" Erica punched her fist in the air. "You speak like a true dragon slayer at last!"

Wiglaf squared his shoulders. He marched through the gatehouse. He started across the drawbridge. Erica and Angus had to run to keep up with him.

"Look!" Angus yelled. He stopped suddenly. "Some strange creature is coming!"

"Creature?" Wiglaf drew his sword. "Never fear! I shall protect you!"

He looked where Angus was pointing. A giant rabbit was hopping toward the drawbridge.

"Run!" the rabbit screamed as it hopped. "Run for your lives!"

Wiglaf stuck his sword back in his belt. It would not do to slay such a helpless creature.

"You heard the rabbit!" Angus cried. "Quick! Into the castle!" He grabbed Wiglaf by the wolf pelt. He tried to drag him back toward the gatehouse.

"Unhand me, man!" Wiglaf cried. He struggled with Angus.

The rabbit hopped closer. Wiglaf saw that it wasn't a rabbit at all. It was a man in a bunny suit.

Erica eyed the rabbit. "Yorick?" she said. "Is that you?"

"It's me," the rabbit said. "I have come to say I was wrong. Seetha won't be here at noon on

Friday. You see, I should have multiplied the wind speed by the width of the smoke cloud. Then divided—"

"Out with it, Yorick!" Wiglaf roared.

"Seetha will be here at noon on *Thursday*," Yorick told them.

"But today is Thursday!" Angus pointed out. "And it's almost noon!"

"Right," Yorick said. "And guess what? Seetha is here!"

Chapter 12

Wiglaf raised his eyes to the sky. Far away, he saw a small, dark cloud. He sniffed the air. Pew! It smelled like rotten eggs.

Wiglaf centered his ram's-horn helmet. He brushed off his wolf pelt. He drew his sword. Then he struck a manly pose on the drawbridge.

"Seetha, you have but little time to live!" Wiglaf roared at the sky. "For I was born to slay you!"

Yorick backed slowly away from Wiglaf. Then he turned and ran across the drawbridge as fast as the legs of his bunny suit would allow. "She's here!" he yelled. "Seetha's here!"

Mordred stuck his head out a tower window. "Seetha's here?" he cried. "Egad!"

"Seetha comes to meet her doom!" Wiglaf called up to the headmaster. "That's me," he added. "*I* am her doom!"

"Oh, right." Mordred rolled his violet eyes. Then he stuck a whistle in his mouth. He blew it until his face was as red as his pajamas, which he still had on.

"Everybody into the castle!" he called. "Hurry now! Step on it, Angus! You, too, Eric!"

"No!" Erica called back. "I shall stay and fight the dragon!"

"Me, too, I guess," said Angus.

Wiglaf looked up. The dark cloud was blowing quickly toward DSA.

"Angus!" Mordred yelled. "Get inside! Do you know what your mother would do to me if I let a dragon get you?"

"Sorry, Wiglaf." Angus shrugged. Then he ran into the castle with surprising speed.

The dark cloud began to drop. Wiglaf saw green smoke puff out from its edges. But its middle was as dark as midnight.

"You, too, Eric!" Mordred yelled. "Inside!"

"No, sir!" Erica cried. "I must fight beside Wiglaf!"

The cloud dropped lower. The smell of rotten eggs grew stronger.

"Into the castle!" Mordred roared. "Now!"

Thunder rumbled from inside the cloud.

"Never!" Erica cried. "I shall not leave my friend in battle! That's Dragon Slayers' Rule #37!"

Once more Mordred's face began to turn as red as his pajamas.

"I *order* you into the castle!" he yelled. "Get in here now! Or turn in the Dragon Slayer of the Month Medal."

Erica gasped. She clutched at her medal.

"Do as he says!" Wiglaf told her. "Seetha is my dragon! This is my fight!"

Erica looked from Wiglaf to Mordred and

back to Wiglaf. "Oh, all right," she said at last. "But take this." She put a small, pointy dagger into Wiglaf's hand. "It's from *The Sir Lancelot Catalog*. It's called Stinger. Good luck, Wiggie!"

So saying, Erica walked sadly across the drawbridge. Wiglaf stuck the dagger into his boot. He stood alone outside the castle. The smoky, smelly, rumbling cloud stopped right over DSA.

"I'm waiting for you, Seetha!" Wiglaf yelled.

The cloud began to drop. Then out of the smoke poked the ugly head of Seetha. Her yellow eyes glowed. Her long tongue flicked out of her mouth. "WAIT NO MORE!" she cried.

Wiglaf gagged as the dragon's breath hit him. It smelled like a garbage dump come to life.

Seetha spread her wings. She flew down from her cloud. She landed beside the moat.

Her smell landed with her. Wiglaf almost

wished Zizmor had changed him into He-Who-Smells-No-Foul-Odors. Seetha was one stinky dragon!

"I AM SEETHA!" the dragon roared. "WHOEVER KILLED MY DARLING BOY—PREPARE TO DIE!"

Chapter 13

"I killed Gorzil!" He-Who-Knows-No-Fear shouted to the dragon.

"YOU?" Seetha drew her lips back from her pointy teeth in what Wiglaf guessed was a smile. "YOU ARE NOT BIG ENOUGH TO KILL A FLEA!"

"I did the deed," Wiglaf yelled. "Me! Wiglaf of Pinwick, Dragon Slayer!"

"THEN TELL ME, WIGLAF, HOW DID GORZIL DIE? LAUGHING AT YOUR SILLY CLOTHES?"

"He died laughing," Wiglaf answered. "Laughing at some jokes I told him. Bad jokes. *Really* bad."

"OH!" Seetha gasped. "YOU GUESSED

HIS SECRET WEAKNESS!" Large orange tears oozed out of her eyes. They rolled down her scaly cheeks. She sniffed. "MY GORZIE WAS EVERYTHING A YOUNG DRAGON SHOULD BE!" she cried. "THE DARLING BOY WAS GREEDY! LAZY! RUDE! CRUEL! HE CHEATED EVERY CHANCE HE GOT! HE WAS...PERFECT!"

Seetha swiped a claw across her runny nose. "BUT ENOUGH CHIT-CHAT!"she roared. "IT'S PAYBACK TIME!"

Seetha flew up and landed on the castle wall. She looked around. Her eyes found Coach Plungett's practice dragon in the castle yard.

"LET ME GIVE YOU A LITTLE DEMON-STRATION! HERE'S A GAME YOU AND I MIGHT PLAY, WIGLAF!" Seetha exclaimed. "SPIT BALL!"

She made a hacking sound in the back of her throat. Up came a blob of fire. She spit it at the straw dragon. WHOOSH! It burst into flames.

Mordred poked his head out of the tower

window. He cupped his hands to his mo

"Excuse me, dragon lady, ma'am?" he called.

Seetha turned toward the window. "AND YOU WOULD BE..."

"Mordred, Your Scaliness. I'm Headmaster of Dragon Sla...um, of this school." He bowed. "Go ahead and have your fun with the boy. But, please. Try not to set the school on fire. I'm afraid that if a spark hits the—"

Seetha cut him off by spitting a fire ball at his head. The headmaster quickly disappeared from the window.

Seetha flew back down to the grass near Wiglaf. "NOW...HOW SHALL I DO YOU IN?" She tapped a claw on her scales, thinking. "WE COULD PLAY BADMINTON—WITH YOU AS THE BIRDIE."

"Whatever, Seetha!" Wiglaf growled. "But I swear by the ram's horns on my helmet that *you* shall be the one to die!" He waved his sword in the air. And with a mighty battle cry he charged at the beast.

Seetha's eyes widened with surprise. Then she blew a puff of red-hot dragon breath right at Wiglaf.

The blast of smelly heat almost knocked Wiglaf off his feet. His wolf pelt crackled. It curled at the edges. Sweat popped out on his brow. But still he ran toward the dragon.

With one claw, Seetha knocked the sword out of Wiglaf's hand. With the other, she struck him. He went rolling head over heels.

Wiglaf came to a stop near the edge of the moat. Before he could get back on his feet, Seetha struck again. She hooked Wiglaf's wolf pelt with her claw. She lifted him up off the ground.

Wiglaf swayed crazily in the air as the dragon lifted him higher and higher. Soon he was face to face with Gorzil's awful mother.

"Back off, smelly one!" Wiglaf cried. "A thousands skunks are not as stinky as you."

Seetha smiled. "Thank you," she said.

Wiglaf was only inches from Seetha's face.

He saw that her scales were covered with dirt and scum. A crust of old, dried slime coated her nose. Her moss-covered fangs had holes in them the size of dinner plates.

"HMMMM...WHAT'S THE *WORST* WAY FOR YOU TO DIE?" Seetha said. "I KNOW! THE TICKLE TORTURE! YOU'LL DIE LAUGHING—JUST LIKE MY GORZIE!"

"Not me!" cried He-Who-Knows-No-Fear. "I can take it!" The dragon's dirty claw came closer and closer to him.

"KITCHY-KITCHY-KOO!" Seetha cried. She tickled Wiglaf's tummy. His neck. His armpits. "KITCHY-KITCHY-KOO!"

But Wiglaf never even smiled.

"NO FAIR! YOU'RE NOT TICKLISH!" Seetha pouted for a minute. "BUT I KNOW MORE GAMES. MANY MORE! LET'S PLAY 'HIGH DIVE'!"

Still clutching Wiglaf, Seetha spread her wings and took off. She landed on the gatehouse roof. She held Wiglaf out, over the moat. "CAN YOU DO A JACKKNIFE WITH A HALF TWIST? HMMMMM?"

Wiglaf looked down. Hundreds of eels looked up at him. They hungrily snapped their jaws.

"You can't scare me, Seetha!" Wiglaf yelled. He drew Erica's dagger from his boot. "For I am He-Who-Knows-No-Fear!"

"OH, YEAH?" the dragon roared. "WELL, I AM SHE-WHO-MAKES-BRAVE-KNIGHTS-CRY-LIKE-BABIES!"

Wiglaf opened his mouth to reply. But a dizzy feeling swept over him. Bright lights flashed. He heard the rush of wind. Seetha's face seemed to melt.

He squeezed his eyes shut.

When he opened them again, the courage spell was broken.

He-Who-Knows-No-Fear was gone.

Now, caught in the dragon's claw was plain old Chicken-Hearted Wiglaf.

Chapter 14

"*Yiiiiiiiiiiiiiiiiiiiiiii!*" screamed Wiglaf. His heart thumped with terror. Any second, Seetha would roast him! Or toast him! Or feed him to the eels!

He tried covering his eyes with his hands. But...what was *this* in his hand?

"MAYBE YOU SHOULD TRY A DOUBLE SOMERSAULT!" Seetha roared. She dangled Wiglaf further out over the moat.

Wiglaf didn't answer. He stared at the dagger. What a sharp, sharp point it had. He could stab Seetha with it. But the very thought made him feel sick. With a shudder, Wiglaf let the dagger slip from his hand.

"*OW!*" Seetha yelped as Stinger stuck her. "MY TOE! MY BEAUTIFUL BIG TOE! WHAT HAVE YOU DONE?"

Seetha tossed Wiglaf away. He sailed through the air. With a thump, he landed on the ground. He bounced twice. Then he lay still.

Above him, the dragon howled in pain. "MY FAVORITE TOE! IT'S BLEEDING!"

Wiglaf moaned. He would be bruised all over. But thanks to Lobelia's heavy leather tunic and thick, quilted breeches, he would live. He pulled himself slowly to his feet.

The dragon rocked back and forth on the gatehouse roof. "LET ME KISS YOU AND MAKE YOU ALL BETTER!" she said to her toe.

Wiglaf glanced up. Seetha held her hurt foot in her front claws. She puckered up her purple lips. With a loud SMACK! she planted a kiss on her toe.

Then Seetha began hopping up and down on her good foot. "I'LL GET YOU, WIGLAF!" she roared. "I'LL MAKE YOU SIZZLE LIKE A FRENCH FRY!"

Wiglaf groaned.

He was a goner!

So Wiglaf did what any chicken-hearted boy would do. He crouched down. He covered his eyes and shook with fear.

"HERE I COME!" Seetha screamed. "I'LL...WHOA! HEY! WHOOO!"

Wiglaf peeked out from behind his fingers.

Seetha teetered on the roof above him. She still held her hurt toe. But something was wrong. Her wings flapped clumsily. Her tail lashed the air. She swayed dangerously back and forth. She lost her balance. Down she plunged.

SPLASH!

Seetha hit the moat.

A huge cloud of steam rose from the waters.

Wiglaf couldn't see a thing.

Suddenly, the dragon lurched up, out of the mist.

Wiglaf jumped back.

"HELP!" Seetha screamed. "HELP ME, YOU FOOLISH BOY!"

But Wiglaf was not *that* foolish.

Seetha kicked and splashed. She slapped the water with her tail.

Wiglaf saw that Seetha's scales looked clean but dull. Her yellow eyes had faded, too. Her horn was drooping to one side. Her tongue hung out the side of her mouth.

"I CAN'T TAKE THIS MUCH LONGER!" Seetha cried. "HELP ME! I'LL GIVE YOU HEAPS OF GOLD!"

Before Wiglaf could shake his head *no*, Mordred leaned out the castle window. "Gold?" he called. "But everyone knows that you have no gold, Seetha!"

"HA!" Seetha laughed. "THAT OLD RUMOR? I'VE GOT MORE GOLD THAN

ANY TEN DRAGONS PUT TOGETHER! AND I HID IT ALL IN THE DARK FOOOOLUB—"

She disappeared under the water again.

Suddenly the drawbridge came down with a bang.

Mordred zoomed out of the castle. He pushed Wiglaf out of the way. He dropped to his knees.

"Seetha!" he cried. "Madam Seetha! Can you hear me?"

"GLUG-GOLD!" Seetha sputtered, popping up. "GET ME OUT OF HERE, BIG BOY— AND IT'S YOURS!"

"Mine?" Mordred gasped as Seetha sank. "Come back, Madam! We have to talk!"

Only Seetha's purple lips popped up now. "GOLBLUB....GLOOOOPH!" The dragon belched and disappeared.

"Hold on, Seetha!" Mordred cried. "I'll save you!" And the headmaster of Dragon Slayers'

Academy dove into the moat to rescue the dragon.

Wiglaf stood alone on the drawbridge. He watched Mordred dive down to find the dragon.

But it was no use.

Seetha's head never again appeared above the dark and murky waters of the moat.

But Mordred's did. "Dragons don't drown!" he cried at last. "How can this be happening?"

Suddenly Wiglaf knew the answer.

"Seetha died from her secret weakness!" he called to the soggy headmaster. "It was a *bath* that killed the beast!"

Wiglaf straightened his ram's-horn helmet.

Then, with his head held high, he walked across the drawbridge and back to DSA.

Mordred stood before all the DSA students in the dining hall that night.

"Did Wiglaf ask Seetha about her gold?" he asked in a hoarse voice.

"Nooooo!" Mordred answered himself. "So I have none of it! Not a single gold coin! All I have—" he sneezed loudly into his red hanky "—is double pneumonia!"

Mordred covered his face with his hands. He began to cry.

"I have some bad news, too," Frypot told the students. The cook made his way to the front of the room.

"When Seetha fell into the moat," he continued, "that filthy dragon poisoned the eels! She killed every single one of them dead."

"What?" Mordred lifted his tear-stained face. "You mean now I have to *buy* groceries to feed all these little gluttons? Oh, this *is* cruel!"

"I'm sorry to tell you this, boys," Frypot went on. "But your days of eating my yummy eel dishes are over."

A hush fell over the great hall.

Then all the students jumped to their feet. They began clapping and stomping and whistling.

Angus shot Wiglaf a thumbs-up sign. "Let's give a cheer for Wiglaf!" he cried.

And they all began to shout. Even Erica, the only DSA student who would actually miss Frypot's eels:

"No more eel! No more eel!
Never again for any meal!
Wiglaf! Wiglaf! He's our man!
If he can do it, anybody can!
Yeaaaaaaaaaaa Wiglaf!"

The students kept clapping and cheering. It warmed Wiglaf's heart. Maybe he hadn't killed Seetha with his sword. Maybe his courage had come from a wizard's spell. But tonight in the DSA dining hall, he was certainly a hero.

~DSA~
YEARBOOK

Goldius est goodius!

The Campus of Dragon Slayers' Academy

DSA

Lady Lobelia's Chamber

Dr. Pluck's Science Lab

Tunnel Exit

Mordred's Classroom

Headmaster's Office

Stabl

Castl Yar

To Dungeon

Dining Hall

Scrubbing Class

Practic Drago

Yorick's Quick Change-O-Rama Camp Site

East Tower

Toenail Village

Huntsman's Path

ir Mort's hoist

Dormitory

Eels Galore Moat

Enter At Your Own Risk

DSA

Drawbridge

~Our Founders~

Sir Herbert Dungeonstone

Sir Ichabod Popquiz

~ Our Philosophy ~

Sir Herbert and Sir Ichabod founded
Dragon Slayers' Academy on a simple
principle still held dear today: Any lad—
no matter how weak, yellow-bellied, lazy,
pigeon-toed, smelly, or unwilling—can be
transformed into a fearless dragon slayer
who goes for the gold. After four years
at DSA, lads will finally be of some
worth to their parents, as well as a
source of great wealth to this distin-
guished academy.* ** ***

* Please note that Dragon Slayers' Academy is a strictly-for-profit
institution.

** Dragon Slayers' Academy reserves the right to keep some of the gold
and treasure that any student recovers from a dragon's lair.

*** The exact amount of treasure given to a student's family is deter-
mined solely by our esteemed headmaster, Mordred. The amount shall be
no less than 1/500th of the treasure and no greater than 1/499th.

Mordred de Marvelous

Mordred graduated from Dragon Bludgeon High, second in his class. The other student, Lionel Flyzwattar, went on to become headmaster of Dragon Stabbers' Prep. Mordred spent years as part-time, semi-substitute student teacher at Dragon Whackers' Alternative School, all the while pursuing his passion for mud wrestling. Inspired by how filthy rich Flyzwattar had become by running a school, Mordred founded Dragon Slayers' Academy in CMLXXIV, and has served as headmaster ever since.

Known to the Boys as: Mordred de Miser
Dream: Piles and piles of dragon gold
Reality: Yet to see a single gold coin
Best-Kept Secret: Mud wrestled under the name Macho-Man Mordie
Plans for the Future: Will retire to the Bahamas . . . as soon as he gets his hands on a hoard

Lady Lobelia

Lobelia de Marvelous is Mordred's sister and a graduate of the exclusive If-You-Can-Read-This-You-Can-Design-Clothes Fashion School. Lobelia has offered fashion advice to the likes of King Felix the Husky and Eric the Terrible Dresser. In CMLXXIX, Lobelia married the oldest living knight, Sir Jeffrey Scabpicker III. That's when she gained the title of Lady Lobelia, but—alas!—only a very small fortune, which she wiped out in a single wild shopping spree. Lady Lobelia has graced Dragon Slayers' Academy with many visits, and can be heard around campus saying, "Just because I live in the Middle Ages doesn't mean I have to look middle-aged."

Known to the Boys as: Lady Lo Lo
Dream: Frightfully fashionable
Reality: Frightful
Best-Kept Secret: Shops at Dark-Age Discount Dress Dungeon
Plans for the Future: New uniforms for the boys with mesh tights and lace tunics

Sir Mort du Mort

Sir Mort is our well-loved professor of Dragon Slaying for Beginners as well as Intermediate and Advanced Dragon Slaying. Sir Mort says that, in his youth, he was known as the Scourge of Dragons. (We're not sure what it means, but it sounds scary.) His last encounter was with the most dangerous dragon of them all: Knight-shredder. Early in the battle, Sir Mort took a nasty blow to his helmet and has never been the same since.

❧

Known to the Boys as: The Old Geezer
Dream: Outstanding Dragon Slayer
Reality: Just plain out of it
Best-Kept Secret: He can't remember
Plans for the Future: Taking a little nap

Coach Wendell Plungett

Coach Plungett spent many years questing in the Dark Forest before joining the Athletic Department at DSA. When at last he strode out of the forest, leaving his dragon-slaying days behind him, Coach Plungett was the most muscle-bulging, physi-cally fit, manliest man to be found anywhere north of Nowhere Swamp. "I am what you call a hunk," the coach admits. At DSA, Plungett wears a number of hats—or, helmets. Besides PE Teacher, he is Slaying Coach, Square-Dance Director, Pep-Squad Sponsor, and Privy Inspector. He hopes to meet a damsel—she needn't be in distress— with whom he can share his love of heavy metal music and long dinners by candlelight.

⚜

Known to the Boys as: Coach
Dream: Tough as nails
Reality: Sleeps with a stuffed dragon named Foofoo
Best-Kept Secret: Just pull his hair
Plans for the Future: Finding his lost lady love

Brother Dave

Brother Dave is the DSA librarian. He belongs to the Little Brothers of the Peanut Brittle, an order known for doing impossibly good deeds and cooking up endless batches of sweet peanut candy. How exactly did Brother Dave wind up at Dragon Slayers' Academy? After a batch of his extra-crunchy peanut brittle left three children from Toenail toothless, Brother Dave vowed to do a truly impossible good deed. Thus did he offer to be librarian at a school world-famous for considering reading and writing a complete and utter waste of time. Brother Dave hopes to change all that.

Known to the Boys as: Bro Dave
Dream: Boys reading in the libary
Reality: Boys sleeping in the library
Best-Kept Secret: Uses Cliff's Notes
Plans for the Future: Copying out all the lyrics to "Found a Peanut" for the boys

Professor Prissius Pluck

Professor Pluck graduated from Peter Piper Picked a Peck of Pickled Peppers Prep, and went on to become a professor of Science at Dragon Slayers' Academy. His specialty is the Multiple Choice Pop Test. The boys who take Dragon Science, Professor Pluck's popular class,

a) are amazed at the great quantities of saliva Professor P. can project

b) try never to sit in the front row

c) beg Headmaster Mordred to transfer them to another class

d) all of the above

Known to the Boys as: Old Spit Face
Dream: Proper pronunciation of *p*'s
Reality: Let us spray
Best-Kept Secret: Has never seen a pippi-hippo-pappa-peepus up close
Plans for the Future: Is working on a cure for chapped lips

Frypot

How Frypot came to be the cook at DSA is something of a mystery. Rumors abound. Some say that when Mordred bought the broken-down castle for his school, Frypot was already in the kitchen and he simply stayed on. Others say that Lady Lobelia hired Frypot because he was so speedy at washing dishes. Still others say Frypot knows many a dark secret that keeps him from losing his job. But no one ever, *ever* says that Frypot was hired because of his excellent cooking skills.

Known to the Boys as: Who needs a nickname with a real name like Frypot?
Dream: Cleaner kitchen
Reality: Kitchen cleaner
Best-Kept Secret: Takes long bubble baths in the moat
Plans for the Future: Has signed up for a beginning cooking class

Yorick

Yorick is Chief Scout at DSA. His knack for masquerading as almost anything comes from his years with the Merry Minstrels and Dancing Damsels Players, where he won an award for his role as the Glass Slipper in "Cinderella". However, when he was passed over for the part of Mama Bear in "Goldilocks", Yorick decided to seek a new way of life. He snuck off in the night and, by dawn, still dressed in the bear suit, found himself walking up Huntsmans Path. Mordred spied him from a castle window, recognized his talent for disguise, and hired him as Chief Scout on the spot.

Known to the Boys as: Who's that?
Dream: Master of Disguise
Reality: Mordred's Errand Boy
Best-Kept Secret: Likes dressing up as King Ken
Plans for the Future: To lose the bunny suit

Wiglaf of Pinwick

Wiglaf, our newest lad, hails from a hovel outside the village of Pinwick, which makes Toenail look like a thriving metropolis. Being one of thirteen children, Wiglaf had a taste of dorm life before coming to DSA and he fit right in. He started the year off with a bang when he took a stab at Coach Plungett's brown pageboy wig. Way to go, Wiggie! We hope to see more of this lad's wacky humor in the years to come.

Dream: Bold Dragon-Slaying Hero
Reality: Still hangs on to a "security" rag
Extracurricular Activities: Animal-Lovers Club, President; No More Eel for Lunch Club, President; Frypot's Scrub Team, Brush Wielder; Pig Appreciation Club, Founder
Favorite Subject: Library
Oft-Heard Saying: *"Ello-hay, Aisy-day!"*
Plans for the Future: To go for the gold!

Angus du Pangus

The nephew of Mordred and Lady Lobelia, Angus walks the line between saying, "I'm just one of the lads" and "I'm going to tell my uncle!" Will this Class I lad ever become a mighty dragon slayer? Or will he take over the kitchen from Frypot some day? We of the DSA Yearbook staff are betting on choice #2. And hey, Angus? The sooner the better!

Dream: A wider menu selection at DSA
Reality: Eel, Eel, Eel!
Extracurricular Activities: DSA Cooking Club, President; Smilin' Hal's Off-Campus Eatery, Sales Representative
Favorite Subject: Lunch
Oft-Heard Saying: *"I'm still hungry"*
Plans for the Future: To write *101 Ways to Cook a Dragon*

Eric von Royale

Eric hails from Someplace Far Away (at least that's what he wrote on his Application Form). There's an air of mystery about this Class I lad, who says he is "totally typical and absolutely average." If that is so, how did he come to own the rich tapestry that hangs over his cot? And are his parents really close personal friends of Sir Lancelot? Did Frypot the cook bribe him to start the Clean Plate Club? And doesn't Eric's arm ever get tired from raising his hand in class so often?

Dream: Valiant Dragon Slayer

Reality: Teacher's Pet

Extracurricular Activities: Sir Lancelot Fan Club; Armor Polishing Club; Future Dragon Slayer of the Month Club; DSA Pep Squad, Founder and Cheer Composer

Favorite Subject: All of Them!!!!!

Oft-Heard Saying: *"When I am a mighty Dragon Slayer . . ."*

Plans for the Future: To take over DSA

Baldrick de Bold

This is a banner year for Baldrick. He is celebrating his tenth year as a Class I lad at DSA. Way to go, Baldrick! If any of you new students want to know the ropes, Baldrick is the one to see. He can tell when you should definitely *not* eat the cafeteria's eel, where the choice seats are in Professor Pluck's class, and what to tell the headmaster if you are late to class. Just don't ask him the answer to any test questions.

Dream: To run the world
Reality: A runny nose
Extracurricular Activities: Practice Dragon Maintenance Squad; Least Improved Slayer-in-Training Award
Favorite Subject: *"Could you repeat the question?"*
Oft Heard Saying: *"A dragon ate my homework."*
Plans for the Future: To transfer to Dragon Stabbers' Prep

～ Advertisements ～